Valerie Fox and the Valentine Box

K.A. Devlin

DEDICATED TO JANICE J,

WHO ALWAYS MADE VALENTINE'S DAY
AND EVERY DAY
SPECIAL

Special thanks to Kenley, Julia, and
Jack for their assistance, patience,
creativity, and love!

Happy Valentine's Day

Valerie Fox was a very nice fox
who lived in a big hollow tree.
On the 14th of February
a message all light and airy,
said "Happy Valentine's Day!"
She was all full of glee!

But she didn't know how
she should celebrate this holiday.
She didn't know what she would need.
Should she hang up some stockings or put up a tree?
Was there something she needed to read?

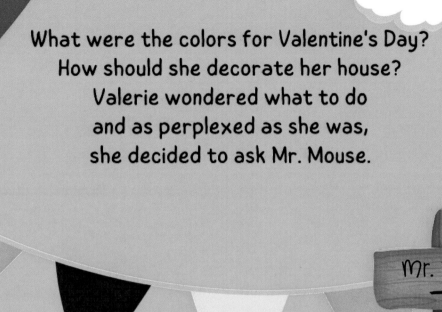

What were the colors for Valentine's Day?
How should she decorate her house?
Valerie wondered what to do
and as perplexed as she was,
she decided to ask Mr. Mouse.

Mr. Mouse

Mrs. Owl

Mrs. Squirrel

So Valerie Fox found a nice little box,
to carry whatever she'd find.
She took the nice box,
tied it up with a string,
and left with her box pulled behind.

Soon Valerie spotted
her friend Mr. Mouse,
while pulling her brown cardboard box.
She had trotted with style,
most nearly a mile,
which was not very far for a fox.

"Why hello there, Miss Fox!
What brings you this way?
I haven't seen you in quite a long while.
I'm so glad that you came!
I hope you feel the same!
Your visits always make me smile!."

"Hello, Mr. Mouse!   I'm here to find out
about Valentine's Day and what I should do.
I know it's a special and fun holiday but
how to celebrate--I haven't a clue."

"Why Miss Fox, I'm so happy
you asked me to help!
I'd love to explain all of the parts!
But to do that, I think,
we should first get Mrs. Owl.
We'll need pie and some
red candy hearts."

So they packed up the treats
and took off for the woods,
looking to meet Mrs. Owl.
Valerie Fox pulled her nice little box.
with the treats wrapped inside with a towel.

They searched up high
and they searched down low
'til they finally heard someone say, "Who?"

"It's me," said the Mouse, "with Valerie Fox.
We've been searching and trying to find you. "

Mr. Mouse said hello to wise Mrs. Owl
and she asked if they'd come a long way.
Mr. Mouse said "not really,
but we've a question to ask.
Can you teach us about this holiday?"

"Valentine's Day? It's a great holiday!
I'd be happy to tell you about it.
Since we have a few hours,
let's get balloons and some flowers
and first go pay Mrs. Squirrel a visit."

So they agreed to go visit Mrs. Squirrel up the hill,
and packed flowers inside of the box.
They went down the road,
balloons floating in tow--
Mr. Mouse, Mrs. Owl, and Miss Fox.

Mrs. Squirrel

Eventually they reached Mrs. Squirrel and her children,
gathering acorns across the hillside.
Mrs. Squirrel said, "Hello,
Mrs. Owl and your friends!
Please join us for some snacks inside!"

"Of course," said Mrs. Owl,
"we'd be happy to join you,
but first I would like you to meet
my friends Mr. Mouse
and Miss Valerie Fox.
We brought you balloons and
some treats."

"Why thank you so much!
You've been so very kind,"
Mrs. Squirrel said with a smile and a nod.
"For these treats we all will surely enjoy
and the balloons we will surely applaud!"

"Mrs. Squirrel, we were hoping to ask you a question,
the answer you must most surely know.
How do we celebrate Valentine's Day?
How does the holiday go?"

"Valentine's Day? What a great holiday!
One that is festive and fun!
I'd be happy to help you
explain how it goes
after our chores are all done."

"We'd be happy to help you with all of your chores,
then we can all have a snack.
We brought flowers and pie
and red candy hearts
We can set it all up when we're back."

So they helped with the chores
and they tidied up a bit,
then they all went to sit in the house.
First Mrs. Squirrel and her children,
then Valerie Fox,
then Mrs. Owl and then dear Mr. Mouse.

"OK," said Mrs. Squirrel as she started to serve
every one with a small piece of pie.
"Let me tell you about
this Valentine's Day,"
and as she said that she let out a sigh.

"Ah Valentine's Day--
A day all about love.
You can see why we think it's so great!
We give hugs and get kisses
from the people we love.
We give cards to our kids and our mate."

"Not just any old cards, these are special, you see.
We call these sweet cards 'valentines.'
We pass them out
to our family and friends,
sometimes we hang them like signs."

"These valentines are filled with our thoughts
and our feelings--
all about how much we love.
We make sure that our loved ones
know how we feel,
so they know how much they are thought of."

"See it's easy to forget on every other day
to tell those who are close that we love them.
But with Valentine's Day
we tell them of our love
and that we know where our love comes from."

"It comes from our heart!
No matter how big or how small.
Our heart is just filled with this love!
Sometimes we forget it
or it seems to get lost,
but Valentine's Day uncovers it all!"

"Oh wow, that's so wonderful,"
said Valerie Fox.
"I think I'm beginning to see!"

"Its easy," said Mrs. Squirrel.
"It's all about love!
Mr. Mouse, Mrs. Owl,
don't you agree?"

"Yes! The valentines we give
to loved ones and friends
are such a big part of the day!
But you're missing another part,
dear Mrs. Squirrel.
We also GET valentines along the way!"

"Wait..what?" asked Valerie.
"We GET valentines too?"

"Oh yes," they all nodded.
"We most certainly do!"

"Ok this is great! Now I know what to do!
I'll make lots of valentines, and I'll give them to you!
I'll draw hearts and I'll color them
in red and in pink,
like the color of real hearts,
I'm starting to think!"

"Just one more thing," said Mrs. Squirrel,
"and it's plain to see.
You've already brought
everything else that you need!"

"You brought us sweet treats
when you came here today--
balloons, flowers, candy, and pies!
On Valentine's Day we share
such sweet treats!
It's always a favorite
surprise!"

"Oh yes!" said Mrs. Owl.
"Mm-hmm," said Mr. Mouse.
"Yessssssss!" the little squirrels squealed.
They each gave Miss Fox a quick hug and a kiss
then ran off to go play in the field.

"With the valentines you'll make,
and the treats that you brought,
your Valentine's Day is almost complete.
The last thing you'll need
is a valentine box
to hold cards and all of your treats!"

"Really? That's it?
Just a valentine box?
I have one! Look and you'll see!"
Valerie held the box up
though now it was empty,
and thought of how fun this would be.

Mrs. Squirrel clapped her hands
and smiled as she said,
"That's it, Valerie! Now you know what to do!
With your valentine box
your quest is complete.
You now know Valentine's Day
through and through!"

The box! Of course!
Look how handy it had been!
She was so glad she brought it, and now could begin.

She would decorate her box with hearts of red and of pink.
She would add some cute flowers too! What do you think?

Valerie

And now it was time to return to her home,
to make valentines for her family and friends.
She just couldn't wait
to begin to celebrate.
She should get there before the day ends.

"Thank you, Mrs. Squirrel.
Thank you Mrs. Owl.
And thank you to dear Mr. Mouse.
I've had such a great time!
You're great friends of mine!
Thanks for inviting me into your house!"

"I've learned so much
about Valentine's Day
and now I'm happy to say
that I wish you all well.
This journey was swell!
I'd like valentines on every day!"

The End

Hope you enjoyed this book! I kindly ask that you please leave a review of it on Amazon. I greatly value your opinion! Your review is so important, plus it will help this book be seen by more customers on Amazon. Please scan the QR code below with your camera for a link to this book listing on Amazon to leave a review. Thank you so much!

For more Valentine's Day fun,
check out these Valentine's Day coloring books, also available on Amazon.

You may also like to check out this book, fun to read any time of the year!

Made in United States
North Haven, CT
07 February 2022

15837342R00027